The Pied Piper of Hamelin

A long time ago, nestled in the foothills of some faraway mountains was the peaceful town of Hamelin. The people of Hamelin were quite content and smug in their happiness. Their bellies were as full as their pockets.

One day, the peaceful town was faced with a big problem—it was overrun by rats!

At first, the rats slunk down sidewalks and slipped through the shadows. But as their numbers grew, they became bold! They scrambled through the streets, invaded villagers' homes, and crawled through every nook and cranny, terrifying people as they went.

Every day there were more rats. Their sharp teeth nibbled and gnawed on everything, and it wasn't long before the villagers' food was running out.

The village was home to many cats, but they were now outnumbered! In an effort solve their rat problem, the villagers set traps and brought in an exterminator. But the rat population kept growing! Something had to be done.

The angry villagers were desperate! They stormed the mayor's office and demanded that something be done to save their town once and for all. The mayor promised to do his best, but the truth was that he didn't really know what to do.

One morning, a strange man who called himself the Pied Piper arrived at the village. He claimed to be a rat catcher and was there to offer his help.

He presented himself before the mayor and claimed that he could rid the village of its rat problem. In return, he asked for his work to be fairly paid. Doubtful that the stranger would accomplish the task, the mayor agreed to pay him if he was successful.

The Pied Piper walked to the center of the village and brought his pipe to his lips. At the very first note he played, rats crept out of their hiding spots and followed the sound of the music, lured by its magical melody.

The Pied Piper toured the village playing his enchanting tune. He walked down each and every lane and passageway. As he carried on, rats by the hundreds scurried to follow behind him in a long line.

The Pied Piper led the rats toward the river. When he reached the riverbank, he stopped and continued to play the pipe. Hypnotized by the magical melody, the rats continued into the water and were carried away by the river's current.

The rat-catching piper returned to the mayor's office, proud to have rid the town of its rats.

"But it was such an easy job! You played a simple melody on your pipe!" scoffed the mayor. "Here, I can offer you one gold coin. Take it or leave it."

The Pied Piper was in disbelief.

"But I did as I said I would!" he protested. "It's only fair to pay me more! Ask your citizens, they'll agree!"

The mayor entered the village square and called upon the villagers. But to the shock and dismay of the Pied Piper, the villagers laughed and scoffed at his request.

Sadly, the Pied Piper left the town, his pockets empty. He decided to teach the mayor and the villagers a lesson.

A few weeks later, everything had returned to normal in the town. The villagers were peacefully going about their daily routines, when they heard the delicate sound of a pipe. The Pied Piper had returned, but this time, the tune was different.

The villagers' children heard the pipe playing and began to joyfully gather around the Pied Piper.

More children joined the growing crowd as the Pied Piper traveled through the village. They laughed and giggled, sang and danced. Soon, all the children of the village were behind him! The Pied Piper led them down a path toward the edge of the village, and then out of the village altogether.

The children's parents couldn't believe their eyes! But they too were mesmerized by the delicate tune, and gazed confusedly after the Pied Piper and the children dancing along the path away from the village.

Over a bridge and toward the mountain they went. The children were so happy and joyful, they continued along the path without a care in the world.

As they reached the foot of the mountain, a cave opened at the sound of the piper's tune. Singing and dancing as they went, the children happily entered the cave one after the other.

When the last child had stepped through the mouth of the cave, the opening to the cave closed and vanished behind him. But there was one child, a boy, whose bad leg had prevented him from keeping up with the others. Because his limp had slowed him down, he had been unable to enter the cave in time.

The boy with the limp turned around and slowly made his way back to the village. He told the villagers where the children had gone, and the parents hurried to the foot of the mountain.

They ran through the woods, but when they reached the spot the boy spoke of, there was only the smooth, solid rock face of the mountain, and no cave to be found!

The parents, the villagers, and the mayor knew what they had to do. They felt terrible about the way they had treated the Pied Piper, and knew that they should apologize to him for mocking him and treating him unfairly. They should have thanked him for his work and paid him properly!

The mayor and the villagers collected coins together and brought them to the foot of the mountain in the same spot where the children had disappeared. Then, they all gathered together behind the mayor.

"Pied Piper!" called out the mayor. "I should have been true to my word! We are very thankful that you rid our town of rats, and are sorry to have treated you unkindly! Here is payment for your work! Please, accept our apology and return our children to us!"

But the mountain was silent. Dismayed, the mayor and the villagers turned toward the village, leaving the coins behind.

While the Pied Piper wanted to teach the villagers a lesson, he was not cruel or unfair.

As the villagers returned home, they heard a faint noise grow louder. It was the sound of children's laughter! Singing and dancing, the children poured into the village square. The villagers had learned their lesson and rejoiced—what a happy day!

Meanwhile, at the foot of the mountain, the Pied Piper smiled and walked toward the sunset, never to be seen nor heard from ever again.